There Is a Carrot in My Ear

HarperTrophy®
A Division of HarperCollinsPublishers

There Is a Carrot in My Ear

and Other Noodle Tales

Retold by Alvin Schwartz
Pictures by
Karen Ann Weinhaus

An I CAN READ Book®

For Nina
and Robert

HarperCollins®, ☂®, Harper Trophy®, and I Can Read Book®
are trademarks of HarperCollins Publishers Inc.

There Is a Carrot in My Ear
and Other Noodle Tales
Text copyright © 1982 by Alvin Schwartz
Illustrations copyright © 1982 by Karen Ann Weinhaus

Library of Congress Cataloging-in-Publication Data
Schwartz, Alvin, date
     There is a carrot in my ear, and other noodle tales.

     (An I can read book)
     Summary: A collection of six stories about a family
of silly people, based on noodle folklore from America,
Europe, and Asia Minor.
     1. Children's stories, America. [1. Humorous
stories] I. Weinhaus, Karen Ann, ill. II. Title.
III. Series.
PZ7.S4Th 1982   [E]   80-8442
ISBN 0-06-025233-2   AACR2
ISBN 0-06-025234-0 (lib. bdg.)
ISBN 0-06-444103-2 (pbk.)

First Harper Trophy edition, 1986.

Contents

Foreword

A noodle is a silly person.
This book is about
a family of noodles
and the silly things
they say and do.

They are Mr. and Mrs. Brown,

and Sam and Jane,

and Grandpa.

1. The Browns
Take the Day Off

It was a hot day.

So Mr. Brown took his family

to the swimming pool.

Sam and Jane jumped right in.

They raced all the way

to the other end

of the pool.

Then they raced back.

Grandpa jumped in.

Then he jumped up and down.

Each time he came down

he called out,

"Brrrrrrrrrrrr!"

11

Mr. Brown bounced up and down
on the diving board.

Mrs. Brown sat in the sun
and turned bright red.

"It is very nice here today,"
said Jane.

"It will be even nicer on Tuesday,"
said the man with the broom.

"Why?" asked Sam.

"Why?" asked Grandpa.

"Why?" asked Mr. Brown.

"Why?" asked Mrs. Brown.

"On Tuesday,"
said the man with the broom,
"there will be water
in the pool."

2. Sam and Jane
Go Camping

Sam and Jane
were camping out.
When it got dark,
they made a big fire
and told stories.

"This is a story

about Bill, the ghost dog,"

said Jane.

"It is a *very* scary story."

"I hope so," said Sam.

"Once upon a time," said Jane,

"there was a big white dog

named Bill.

Bill had a very mean owner.

He wouldn't feed Bill

or pet him

or anything.

Then one night—"

Suddenly Jane stopped.

She heard a strange sound.

Hmmmmmmmm!

Hmmmmmmmmmmmmmm!

HMMMMMMMMMMMMMMMM!

It was getting louder

and louder.

"Ouch!" cried Sam.

"Something bit me!"

"Ouch!" yelled Jane.

"Something bit me, too!"

21

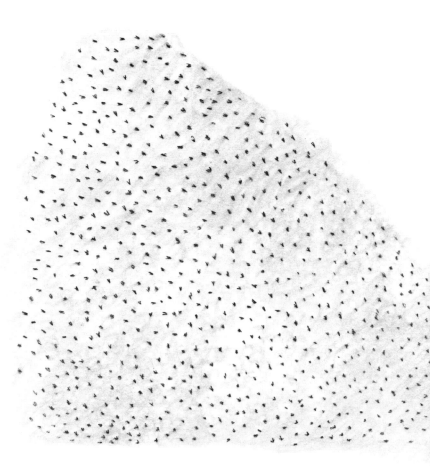

"It's a bunch of mosquitoes!"

yelled Sam.

They jumped up and down

and ran around

and waved their arms.
But the mosquitoes
would not go away.
"Let's put out the fire,"
whispered Sam.
"They'll never find us
in the dark."

They put out the fire

and sat down on a rock.

A mosquito flew by,

then disappeared.

It was as quiet as a graveyard.

"They are gone!"

whispered Jane.

"I think so,"

whispered Sam.

Then some fireflies flew by.

"Oh, no!" Sam groaned.

"They are back!

And now they are looking for us

with flashlights."

3. Mr. Brown

Washes His Underwear

On Saturday

Mr. Brown washed

his dirty clothes.

He washed his socks,

his shirts,

and his underwear.

28

Then he hung them up to dry
in the backyard.
He hung the underwear
in the apple tree.

When the wind blew,

the underwear waved its arms

and kicked its legs.

It looked like a dancing ghost.

31

After supper that night,

Mrs. Brown looked out the window.

"There is a man in the apple tree,"

she told Mr. Brown.

"Don't worry," he said.

"I will scare him away."

Mr. Brown went into the yard.

He called out,

"Who are you?

What do you want?"

Nobody answered.

He called out again,

"Who are you?

What do you want?"

Again nobody answered.

34

Mr. Brown got angry.

"You are *very* rude

not to answer me,"

he shouted.

But still there was no answer.

So Mr. Brown picked a ripe tomato,

and he threw it

at the man in the tree.

Then he threw another—

and another,

and another.

"*That* will show you!" he shouted.

The next morning,

he went outside

to get his clothes.

When he got to the apple tree,

he was very surprised.

His underwear was covered

with squashed tomatoes,

and it was dripping

tomato juice.

"I am really lucky

I wasn't wearing

that underwear,"

Mr. Brown said to himself.

4. Jane Grows a Carrot

Jane and Sam

were walking home

from school.

"I have a secret to tell you,"
said Jane.

"I won't tell anybody,"
said Sam.

"There is a carrot in my ear,"
said Jane.
"It has been growing there
all week."

"That is *very* strange," said Sam.

"How did that happen?"

"I don't know," said Jane.

"I planted radishes."

5. Grandpa Buys
a Pumpkin Egg

After breakfast

Grandpa took a long walk.

In front of the grocery store

he saw a big pile of pumpkins.

"What are those big round things?"

he asked the grocer.

44

"Don't you know?"

the grocer asked him.

"I don't think so,"

said Grandpa.

The grocer smiled.

"They are horse eggs," he said.

"You put one in a sunny place

and sit on it for a day

and a night,

and it will hatch

a baby horse."

"I bet Sam would like one!"

Grandpa thought.

"Okay," he said,

"give me the biggest one."

When Grandpa got home,

he put the pumpkin

in the backyard.

Then he went into the kitchen

and got

a chicken leg,

a hard-boiled egg,

some jelly beans,

and some lemonade.

"Now I won't get hungry,"

he said to himself.

Then he sat on the pumpkin,

and he waited.

He sat all that day,

and he sat all that night.

By the next morning

he was so tired

he fell asleep

and fell off the pumpkin.

When that happened,

the pumpkin started rolling

down the hill.

It rolled and it rolled

until it crashed

into a bush.

A rabbit was sitting

inside the bush.

When the pumpkin rolled in,

the rabbit jumped out

and started running.

Grandpa saw the rabbit,

and he got very excited.

"Come back, little horse!"

he called.

"Come back!"

But the rabbit kept running.

Grandpa went to see the grocer again.

"I want my money back," he said.

"Why?" asked the grocer.

"Well," said Grandpa,

"the egg hatched all right.

But the baby horse ran away."

6. It Is Time
to Go to Sleep

"It is ten o'clock,"

Mrs. Brown called out.

"Time to go to sleep!"

"I am taking my ruler to bed,"
said Sam.

"I want to know

how long I sleep."

"I am taking my bicycle to bed,"
said Jane.
"I am tired of walking
in my sleep."

"I am taking

my running shoes to bed,"

said Mr. Brown.

"Last night I dreamed

a bear was chasing me,

and I don't want him

to catch me."

"I am taking my mirror to bed,"
said Grandpa.
"I want to see how I look
when I'm asleep."

Then Mr. Brown

said to Mrs. Brown,

"Put the light out

and come to bed."

So Mrs. Brown

put the light out

and came to bed.

And they all went to sleep.

Author's Note

Each of the tales in this book is based on an older noodle tale.

"The Browns Take the Day Off" is from an American "Little Moron" story of the 1940s and 1950s.

"Sam and Jane Go Camping" is from a firefly tale told in Europe and America.

"Mr. Brown Washes His Underwear" is based on a story about the famous Turkish noodle Khoja Nasreddin.

"Jane Grows a Carrot" is from an American vaudeville joke.

"Grandpa Buys a Pumpkin Egg" is based on "The Mare's Egg," a traditional tale told in Europe and America.

"It Is Time to Go to Sleep" is drawn from five noodle tales. "The Ruler" and "The Bicycle" are from "Little Moron" stories. "The Dream" is an ancient Greek tale. "The Mirror" and "Putting the Light Out" are told in Europe and America.